CALGARY PUBLIC LIBRARY

SEP _ _ 2016

DAYDREAMING

MARK TATULLI

CK
Tick
TICK TICK
TICK TICK BBBBRRRRRIIIIIIIIIINNNNGGGGGG

Roaring Brook Press

New York

Rise and shine, Henry!

Let's get moving!

BBBBRRIINNG!

For Donna

Copyright © 2016 by Mark Tatulli
Published by Roaring Brook Press
Roaring Brook Press is a division of Holtzbrinck
Publishing Holdings Limited Partnership
175 Fifth Avenue, New York, New York 10010

mackids.com

Library of Congress Control Number: 2016932187

ISBN: 978-1-62672-354-2

Our books may be purchased in bulk for promotional, educational, or business use. Please contact your local bookseller or the
Macmillan Corporate and Premium Sales Department at (800) 221-7945 ext. 5442 or by e-mail at MacmillanSpecialMarkets@macmillan.com.

First edition 2016
Book design by Andrew Arnold
Printed in China by Toppan Leefung Printing Ltd., Dongguan City, Guangdong Province

10 9 8 7 6 5 4 3 2 1